A MESSAGE TO PARENTS

It is of vital importance for parents to read good books to young children in order to aid the child's psychological and intellectual development. At the same time as stimulating the child's imagination and awareness of his environment, it creates a positive relationship between parent and child. The child will gradually increase his basic vocabulary and will soon be able to read books alone.

Brown Watson has published this series of books with these aims in mind. By collecting this inexpensive library, parent and child are provided with hours of pleasurable and profitable reading.

SNOWY
The Christmas Snowman

Text by Maureen Spurgeon

Brown Watson
ENGLAND

"Cold enough for snow!" said Simon and Julie's dad, taking one last look out at their back garden before locking the door for the night.

"I hope not!" said Mum, who was busy baking. "I hate Christmas shopping when it snows."

All the same, Simon and Julie couldn't help wishing that it WOULD snow – even if it was just enough to build a snowman for Christmas! And when they woke up next day – what do you think?

Roofs of houses and garden sheds, window sills and fences were powdered with snow, sparkling in the winter sunshine like icing sugar. "Great!" Simon cried. "We can build a snowman."

"You'll have to be quick!" laughed
Dad. "We didn't have much snow,
and it won't last long."
"Good!" said Mum, mixing the
cake. "I'm glad," added Gran.

The children put on their coats, wellingtons, woolly hats and gloves and went outside. "It's true what Dad says," sighed Julie looking around. "There isn't really all that much snow . . ."

"I think there's enough by the wall," Simon told her, scooping up quite a few handfuls. "See if you can make a big snowball for the head, and I'll start on the snowman's body."

Julie found that getting enough snow to make even a little snowball was not easy. Scraping the whole of the garden fence only gave her a tiny handful, and most of that was already melting.

Simon had not done much better with the snowman's body. And if Mum hadn't opened an upstairs window, sending down a shower of snow, they would not have managed to finish him, at all.

"He's a bit small . . ." said Julie. "Don't worry!" said Simon. "We can always make him bigger, as long as we get some more snow before Christmas. Let's call him Snowy, the Christmas Snowman!"

The weather stayed quite cold,
but there was no more snow.
"At least I can hang out some
washing," said Mum.
"And I can do some Christmas
shopping," smiled Gran.

Julie and Simon were very disappointed.

"Oh, don't worry about your snowman," Dad told them. "That wall gets hardly any sun, you know. He'll last until Christmas."

But there was no mistake about it. Snowy was getting smaller and smaller. And the smaller he got, the easier it became for the pale, winter sun to melt more and more of him away.

If it had not been for Jack Frost coming round every night and touching everything with his long, icy fingers, Snowy knew he would never have lasted so long.

Everyone else seemed so happy. Fairy lights appeared in all the windows, and Snowy could hear Simon and Julie laughing and chatting as they helped to put up the decorations.

"Time to mix the Christmas pudding!" came Mum's voice. "Take it in turns to make a wish!" "I'd wish to be a real Christmas snowman!" thought Snowy.

Snowy glanced up at the dark sky, hoping he'd see clouds gathering around, hiding the moon before the first snowflakes drifted down. Instead, it was a clear night, with lots of stars.

He looked again. Something was gliding towards the moon, something piled high, with a man in boots and a hood, pulled by animals with what looked like tree branches on their heads . . .

"Reindeer . . ." whispered Snowy. Simon and Julie had talked a lot about Santa Claus and what they hoped he would bring them on his sleigh. Snowy knew he came from a land of ice and snow . . .

"I wish Santa Claus could bring
me some snow," thought poor
Snowy. He closed his eyes tight,
not wanting to see anything to
remind him of the happy time
Christmas was meant to be.
At first, Snowy thought he was

dreaming. Something soft began falling on his face, his head, then his body, fluttering all around him like a shower of bright moonbeams, making him feel warm and happy . . .

"Snow!" cried Snowy joyfully. "Merry Christmas!" came the cry from above. "Merry Christmas, Snowy!" And in a final burst of stars and moonbeams, both reindeer and sleigh were gone.

"Well, I got just what I wanted for Christmas," said Dad in his new dressing gown. "So did we!" cried Julie and Simon. "Except for our Christmas snowman," added Julie solemnly.

"Well," said Grandma, standing at the back door, "I don't know about that. See for yourselves, you two!" Simon and Julie looked at each other, sure that there had been no snow at all.

Snowy, the Christmas snowman stood proud and tall. His head was round and jolly, and his body so plump and cuddly that Julie could not help giving him a hug for Christmas morning.